DINOSAURS WITH JOBS
a coloring book celebrating
our old-school coworkers

drawn and written by
Theo Nicole Lorenz

ISBN 978-1492849285

Disclaimer: A few of the creatures shown in this book are not, technically speaking, dinosaurs. Plesiosaurus and ichthyosaurus are prehistoric marine reptiles, and pterodactyl is a prehistoric flying reptile. The artist apologizes for any confusion caused by their inclusion.

Disclaimer 2: The artist is not actually sorry for including them, though, because they're awesome and were super fun to draw.

Disclaimer 3: You probably shouldn't be relying on coloring books about dinosaur employment for your scientific education, anyway. Go to the library.

Dinosaurs are an important part of our workforce.

Stegosaurus works in a clothing store and enjoys being helpful.

Argentinosaurus is one of the world's largest dinosaurs and the world's largest driving instructor.

Dilophosaurus is a classically trained Shakespearean actor.

Plesiosaurus tech support specialist would like to remind you that the CD drive is NOT a cupholder.

Ankylosaurus's band is going to make it big any day now.

Being a stay-at-home parent is rewarding,
but Parasaurolophus wishes it came with paid time off.

Iguanodon is a celebrity chef with his own reality TV show.

Ornithomimus works the drive-thru window
and gets all the fried chicken she can eat.

Pachycephalosaurus uses empathy instead of head-butting to help clients at her therapy practice.

Spinosaurus loves working with animals
at the pet grooming shop!

Despite the fact that she can't actually fit inside a house,
Apatosaurus is one of the top real estate agents in the area.

Velociraptor teaches the most well-behaved
kindergarten class this school has ever seen.

Allosaurus has been even more of a show-off
since he landed his big pro basketball contract.

Compsognathus channeled his enthusiasm and flair
into a career as a wedding planner.

Ichthyosaurus found her dream job:
working as a lifeguard at the local pool.

Ampelosaurus balances a career in accounting
with a punk rock lifestyle.

Protoceratops is the first Cretaceous creature in space!

Everyone told Tyrannosaurus he could never be a waiter because of his little arms, but he makes it work.

Pterodactyl is unemployed at the moment,
so she's applying for jobs and watching crime dramas.

About the Artist

Theo is an artist, writer, and coloring book tycoon who lives in Saint Paul, Minnesota with her stegosaurus assistant, Steve. She has an MFA in creative writing from Hamline University.

Dinosaurs With Jobs is her third coloring book, following Fat Ladies in Spaaaaace: a body-positive coloring book and Unicorns Are Jerks: a coloring book exposing the cold, hard, sparkly truth.

This book is dedicated to Teri and Ty, Compsognathus's favorite clients.